[redacted]

VADER: VOLUME 4

Chaos grips the Galactic Empire. After the destruction of THE DEATH STAR, the disgraced Sith Lord, DARTH VADER was demoted by his Master, Emperor Palpatine. It is now clear to him that no man can be trusted. The rule of law is in danger.

Unknown to the Emperor, Vader is quietly pursuing his own interests: the mysterious Force-strong pilot who destroyed the Death Star and the identity of the stranger who is conspiring with the Emperor.

But for this he will need his own personal, secret forces. Vader recruits droid archaeologist DOCTOR APHRA to do so - and she leads the fallen Jedi to the old warzone of GEONOSIS....

KIERON GILLEN
Writer

SALVADOR LARROCA
Artist

EDGAR DELGADO
Colorist

VC's JOE CARAMAGNA
Letterer

ADI GRANOV
Cover Artist

HEATHER ANTOS & CHARLES BEACHAM
Assistant Editors

JORDAN D. WHITE
Editor

C.B. CEBULSKI & MIKE MARTS
Executive Editors

AXEL ALONSO
Editor In Chief

JOE QUESADA
Chief Creative Officer

DAN BUCKLEY
Publisher

For Lucasfilm:
Senior Editor JENNIFER HEDDLE
Creative Director MICHAEL SIGLAIN
Lucasfilm Story Group RAYNE ROBERTS, PABLO HIDALGO, LELAND CHEE

ABDO
Spotlight

ABDOPUBLISHING.COM

Reinforced library bound edition published in 2017 by Spotlight,
a division of ABDO, PO Box 398166, Minneapolis, Minnesota 55439.
Spotlight produces high-quality reinforced library bound editions for
schools and libraries. Published by agreement with Marvel Characters, Inc.

Printed in the United States of America, North Mankato, Minnesota.
042016
092016

THIS BOOK CONTAINS
RECYCLED MATERIALS

marvelkids.com

STAR WARS © & TM 2016 LUCASFILM LTD.

PUBLISHER'S CATALOGING IN PUBLICATION DATA

Names: Gillen, Kieron, author. | Larroca, Salvador ; Delgado, Edgar, illustrators.
Title: Vader / by Kieron Gillen ; illustrated by Salvador Larroca and Edgar Delgado.
Description: Minneapolis, MN : Spotlight, [2017] | Series: Star Wars : Darth Vader
Summary: Follow Vader straight from the ending of A New Hope into his own solo
     adventures-showing the Empire's war with the Rebel Alliance from the other
     side! When the Dark Lord needs help, to whom can he turn?
Identifiers: LCCN 2016932362 | ISBN 9781614795209 (v.1 : lib. bdg.) | ISBN
     9781614795216 (v. 2 : lib. bdg.) | ISBN 9781614795223 (v. 3 : lib. bdg.) | ISBN
     9781614795230 (v. 4 : lib. bdg.) | ISBN 9781614795247 (v.5 : lib. bdg.) | ISBN
     9781614795254 (v. 6 : lib. bdg.)
Subjects: LCSH: Vader, Darth (Fictitious character)--Juvenile fiction. | Star Wars
     fiction--Comic books, strips, etc.--Juvenile fiction. | Graphic novels--Juvenile
     fiction.
Classification: DDC 741.5--dc23
LC record available at http://lccn.loc.gov/2016932362

Spotlight

A Division of ABDO
abdopublishing.com

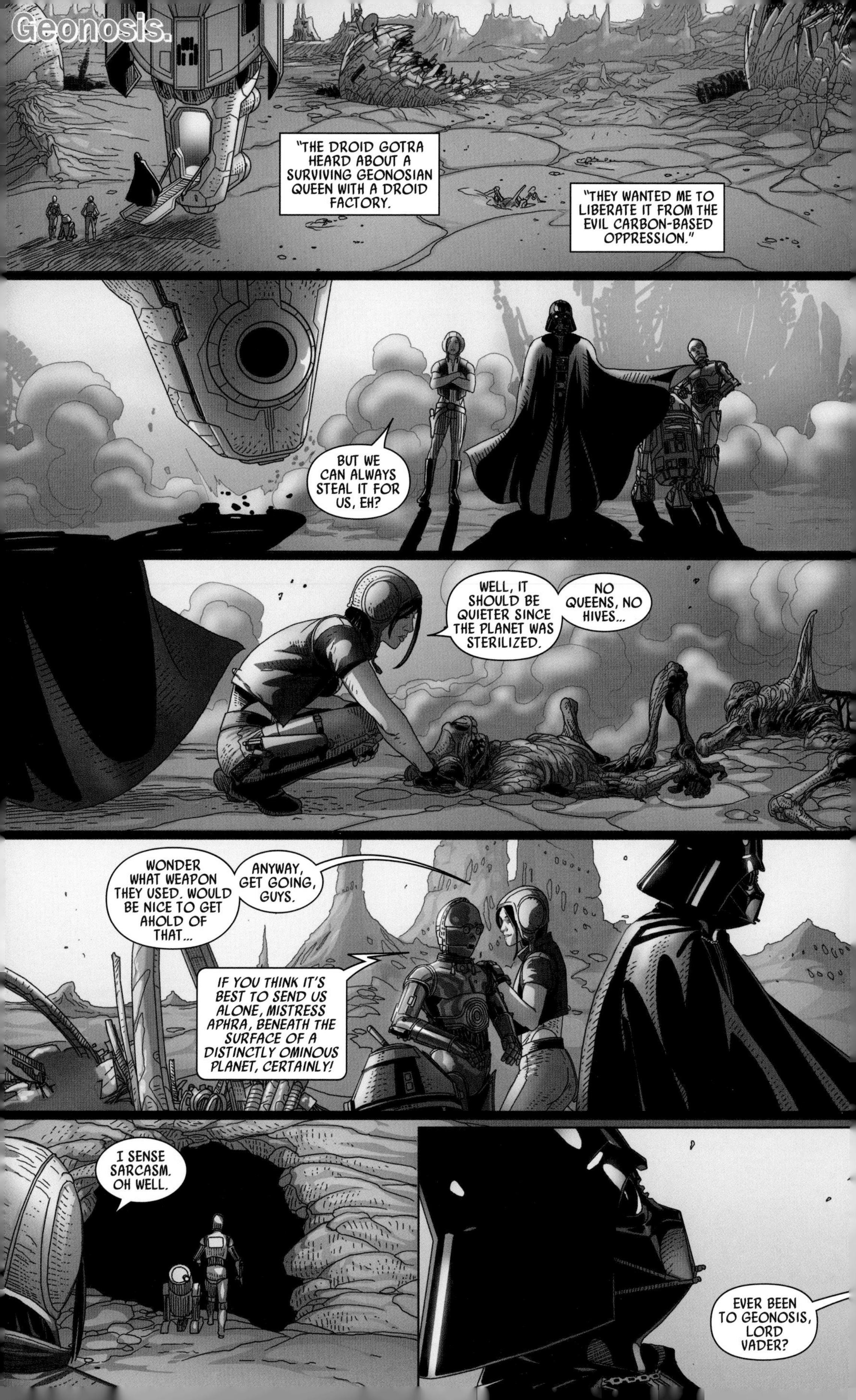
Geonosis.
"THE DROID GOTRA HEARD ABOUT A SURVIVING GEONOSIAN QUEEN WITH A DROID FACTORY.
"THEY WANTED ME TO LIBERATE IT FROM THE EVIL CARBON-BASED OPPRESSION."
BUT WE CAN ALWAYS STEAL IT FOR US, EH?
WELL, IT SHOULD BE QUIETER SINCE THE PLANET WAS STERILIZED.
NO QUEENS, NO HIVES...
WONDER WHAT WEAPON THEY USED. WOULD BE NICE TO GET AHOLD OF THAT...
ANYWAY, GET GOING, GUYS.
IF YOU THINK IT'S BEST TO SEND US ALONE, MISTRESS APHRA, BENEATH THE SURFACE OF A DISTINCTLY OMINOUS PLANET, CERTAINLY!
I SENSE SARCASM. OH WELL.
EVER BEEN TO GEONOSIS, LORD VADER?

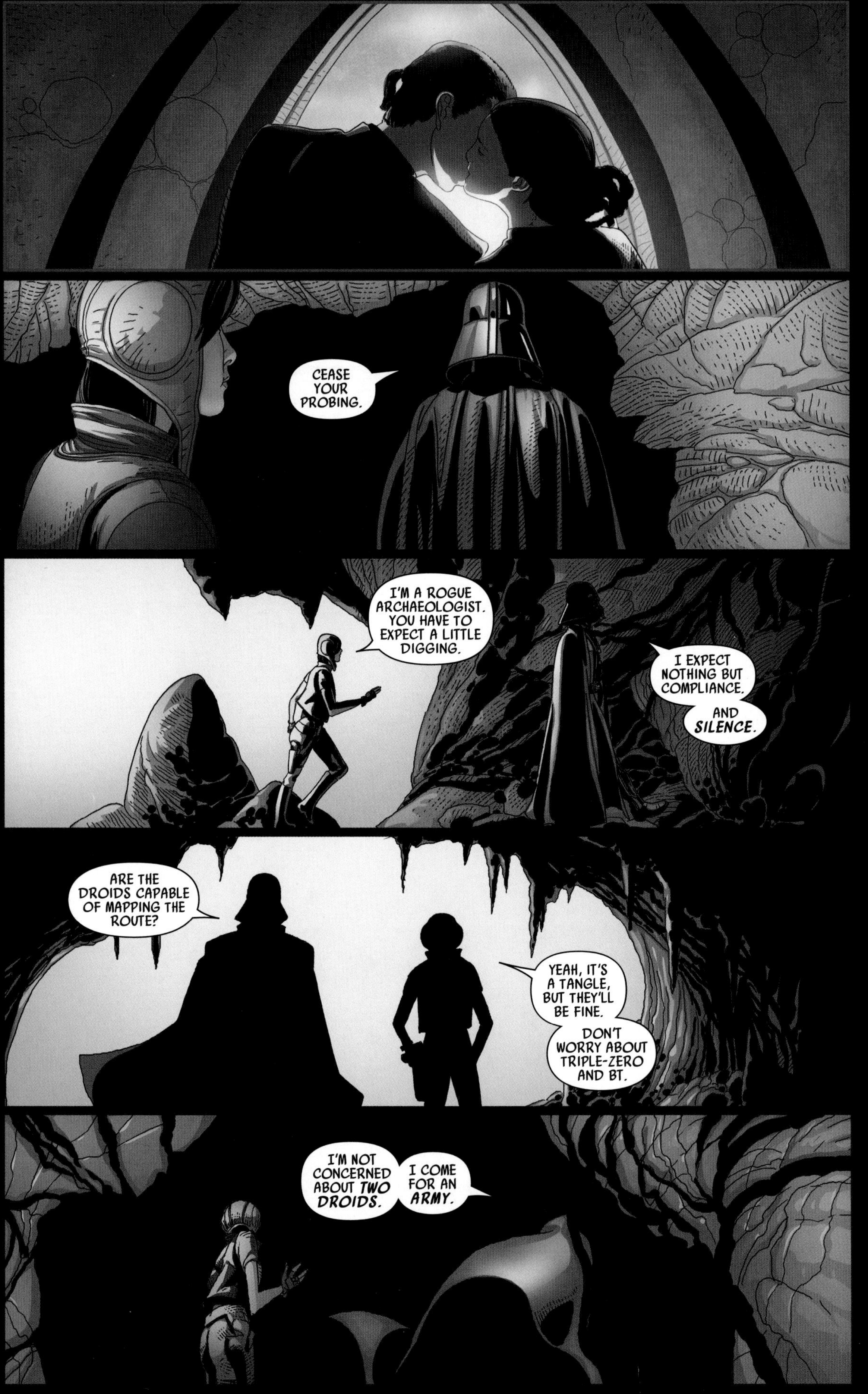
CEASE YOUR PROBING.
I'M A ROGUE ARCHAEOLOGIST. YOU HAVE TO EXPECT A LITTLE DIGGING.
I EXPECT NOTHING BUT COMPLIANCE.
AND SILENCE.
ARE THE DROIDS CAPABLE OF MAPPING THE ROUTE?
YEAH, IT'S A TANGLE, BUT THEY'LL BE FINE.
DON'T WORRY ABOUT TRIPLE-ZERO AND BT.
I'M NOT CONCERNED ABOUT TWO DROIDS.
I COME FOR AN ARMY.

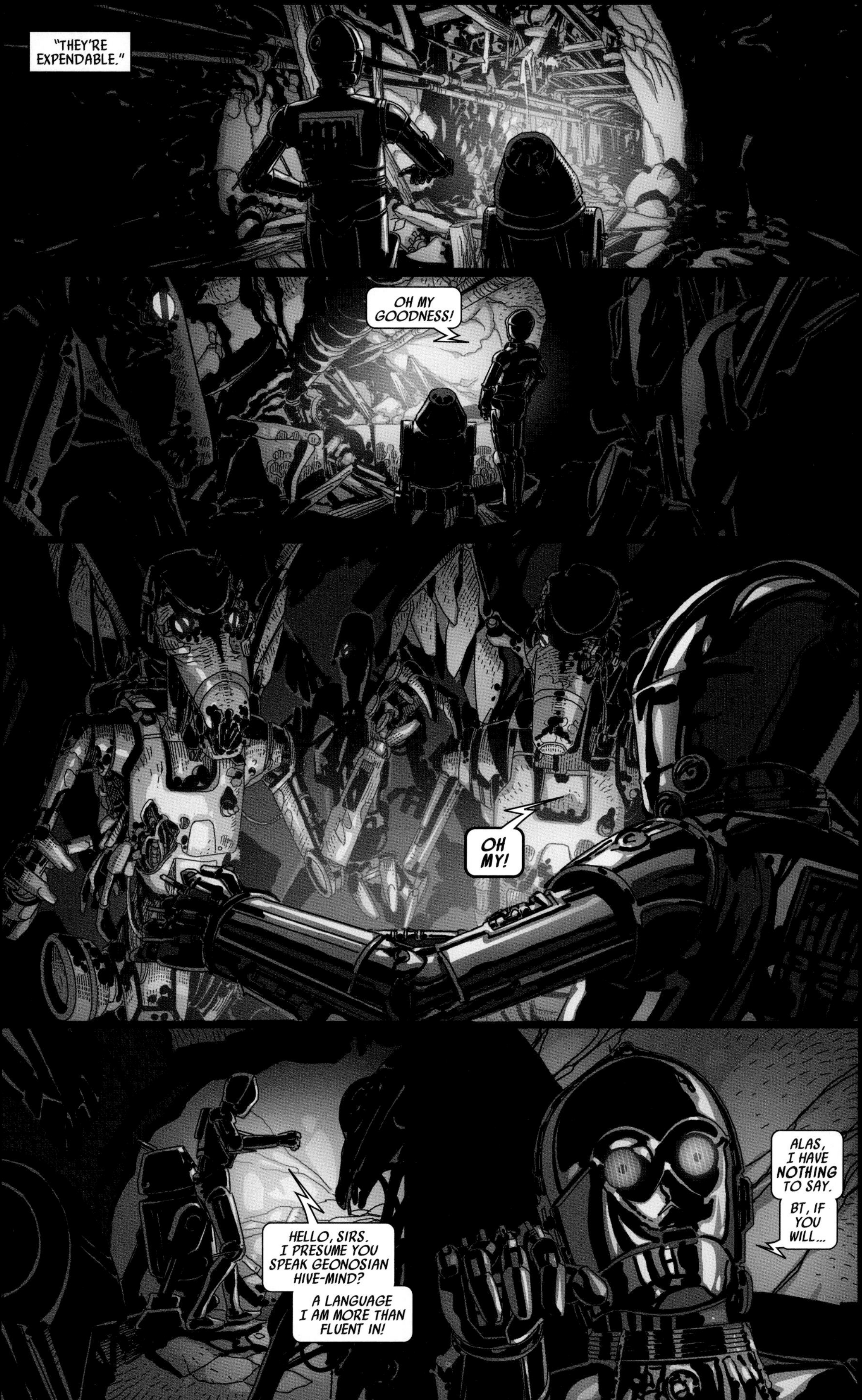
"THEY'RE EXPENDABLE."
OH MY GOODNESS!
OH MY!
HELLO, SIRS. I PRESUME YOU SPEAK GEONOSIAN HIVE-MIND?
A LANGUAGE I AM MORE THAN FLUENT IN!
ALAS, I HAVE NOTHING TO SAY.
BT, IF YOU WILL...

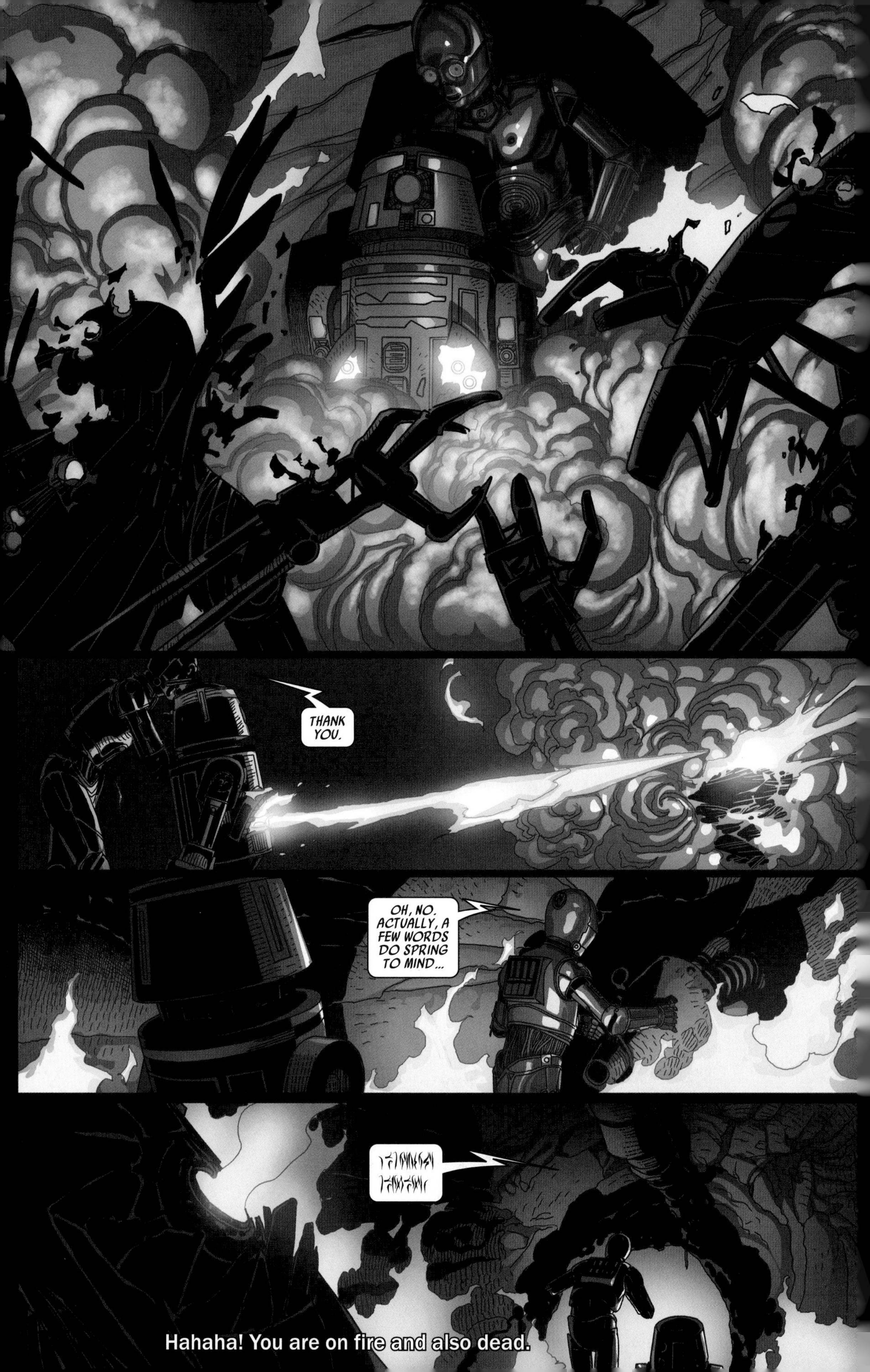
THANK YOU.
OH, NO. ACTUALLY, A FEW WORDS DO SPRING TO MIND...
Hahaha! You are on fire and also dead.

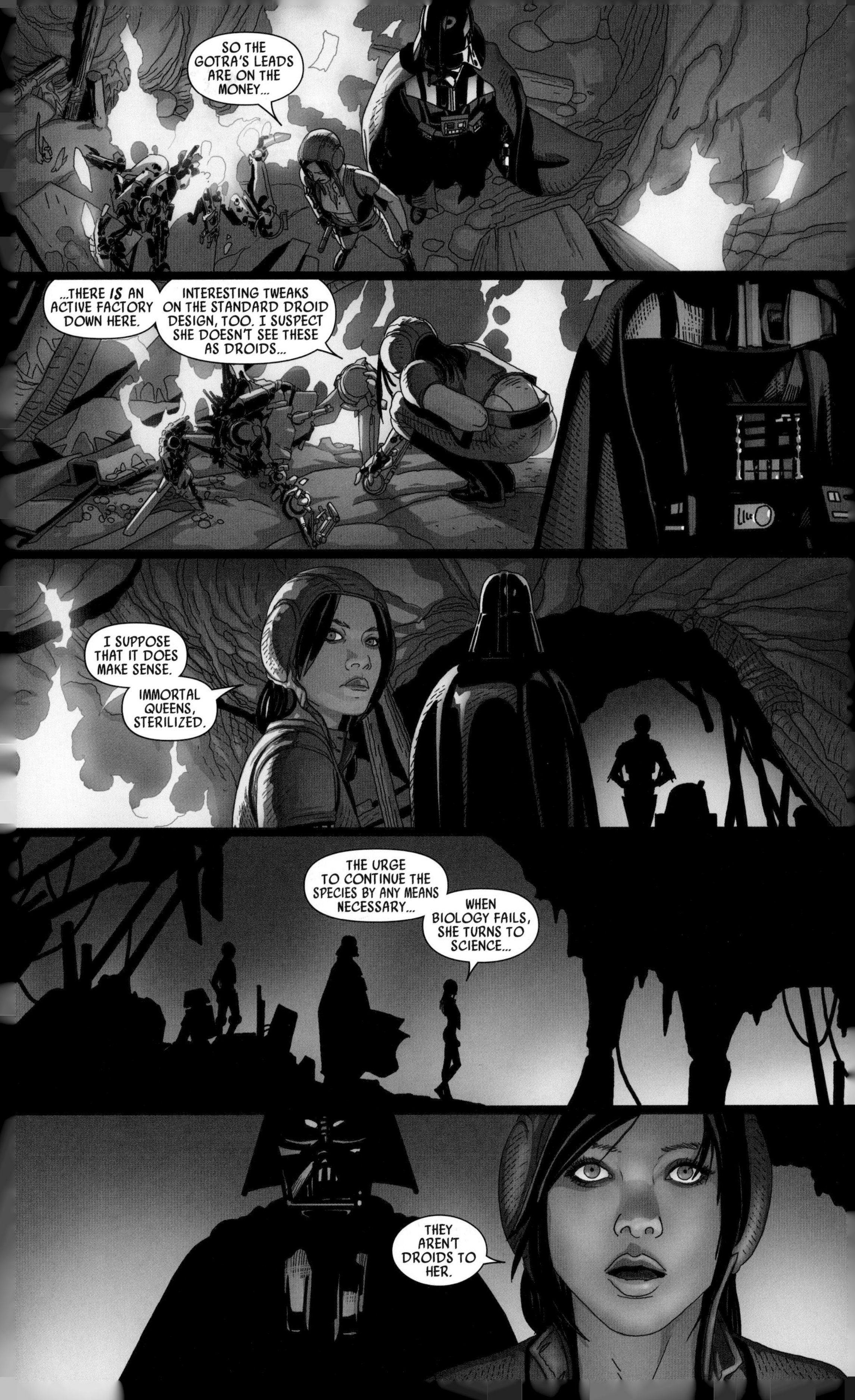
SO THE GOTRA'S LEADS ARE ON THE MONEY...
...THERE *IS* AN ACTIVE FACTORY DOWN HERE.
INTERESTING TWEAKS ON THE STANDARD DROID DESIGN, TOO. I SUSPECT SHE DOESN'T SEE THESE AS DROIDS...
I SUPPOSE THAT IT DOES MAKE SENSE.
IMMORTAL QUEENS, STERILIZED.
THE URGE TO CONTINUE THE SPECIES BY ANY MEANS NECESSARY...
WHEN BIOLOGY FAILS, SHE TURNS TO SCIENCE...
THEY AREN'T DROIDS TO HER.

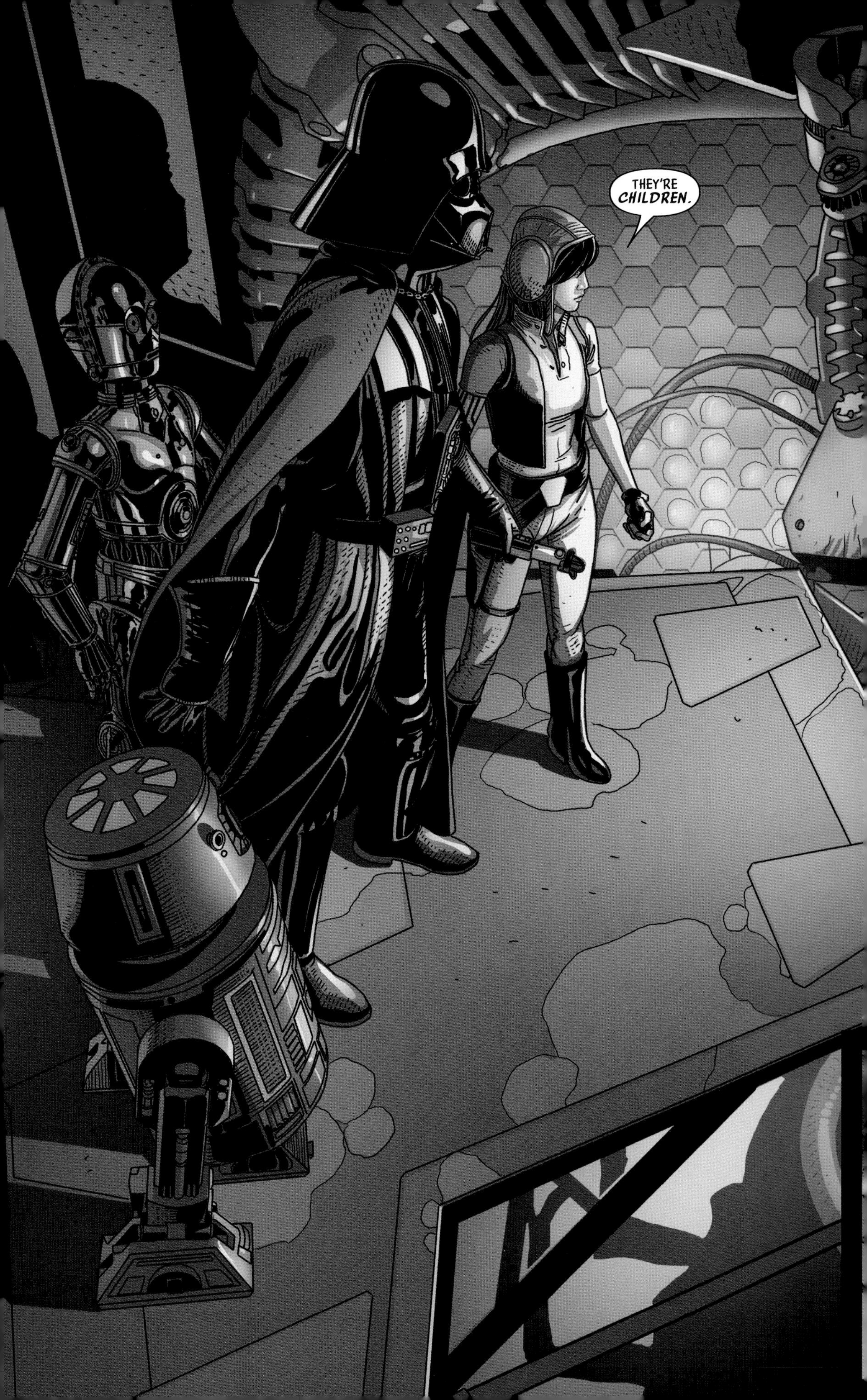
THEY'RE CHILDREN.

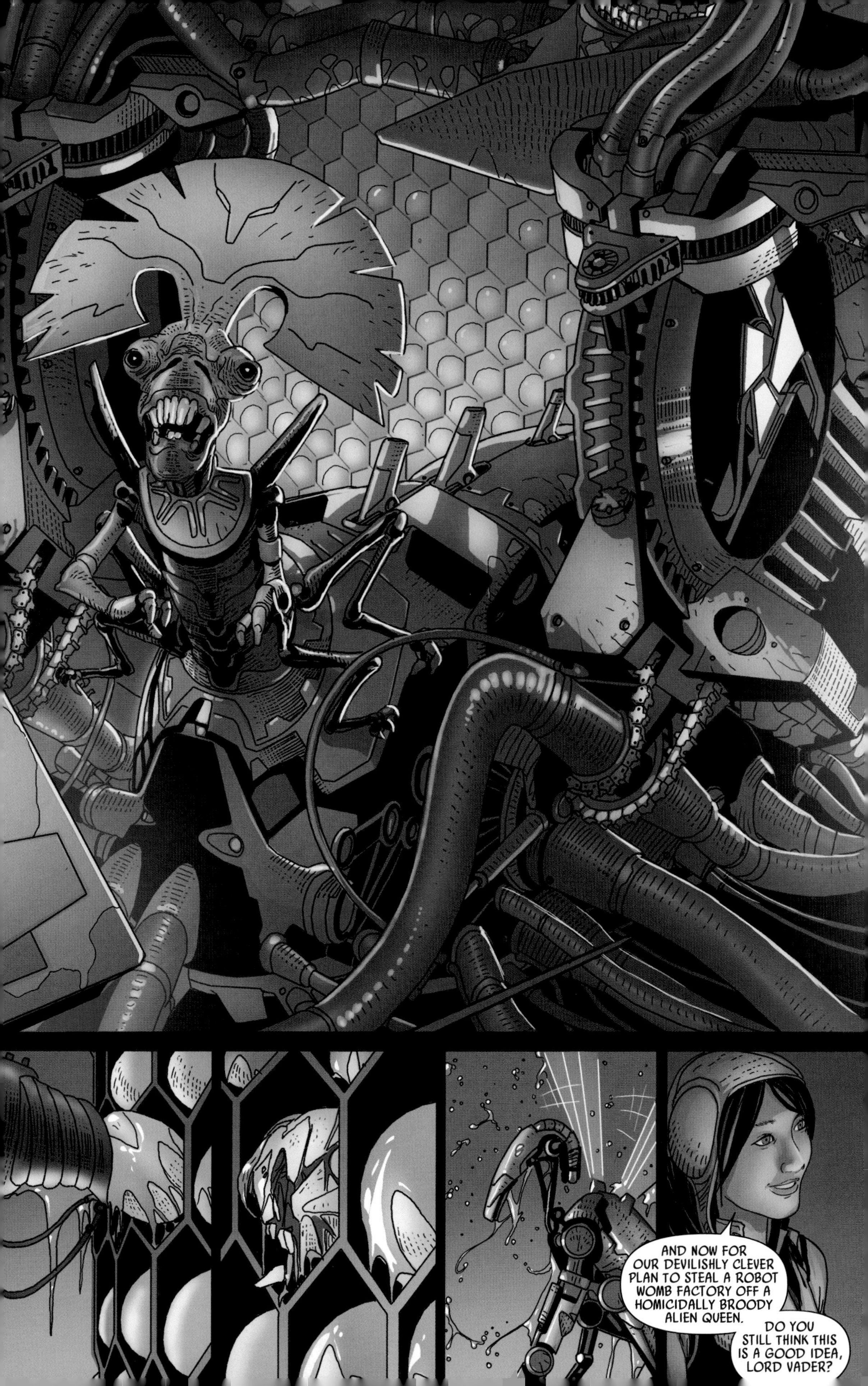
AND NOW FOR OUR DEVILISHLY CLEVER PLAN TO STEAL A ROBOT WOMB FACTORY OFF A HOMICIDALLY BROODY ALIEN QUEEN.
DO YOU STILL THINK THIS IS A GOOD IDEA, LORD VADER?

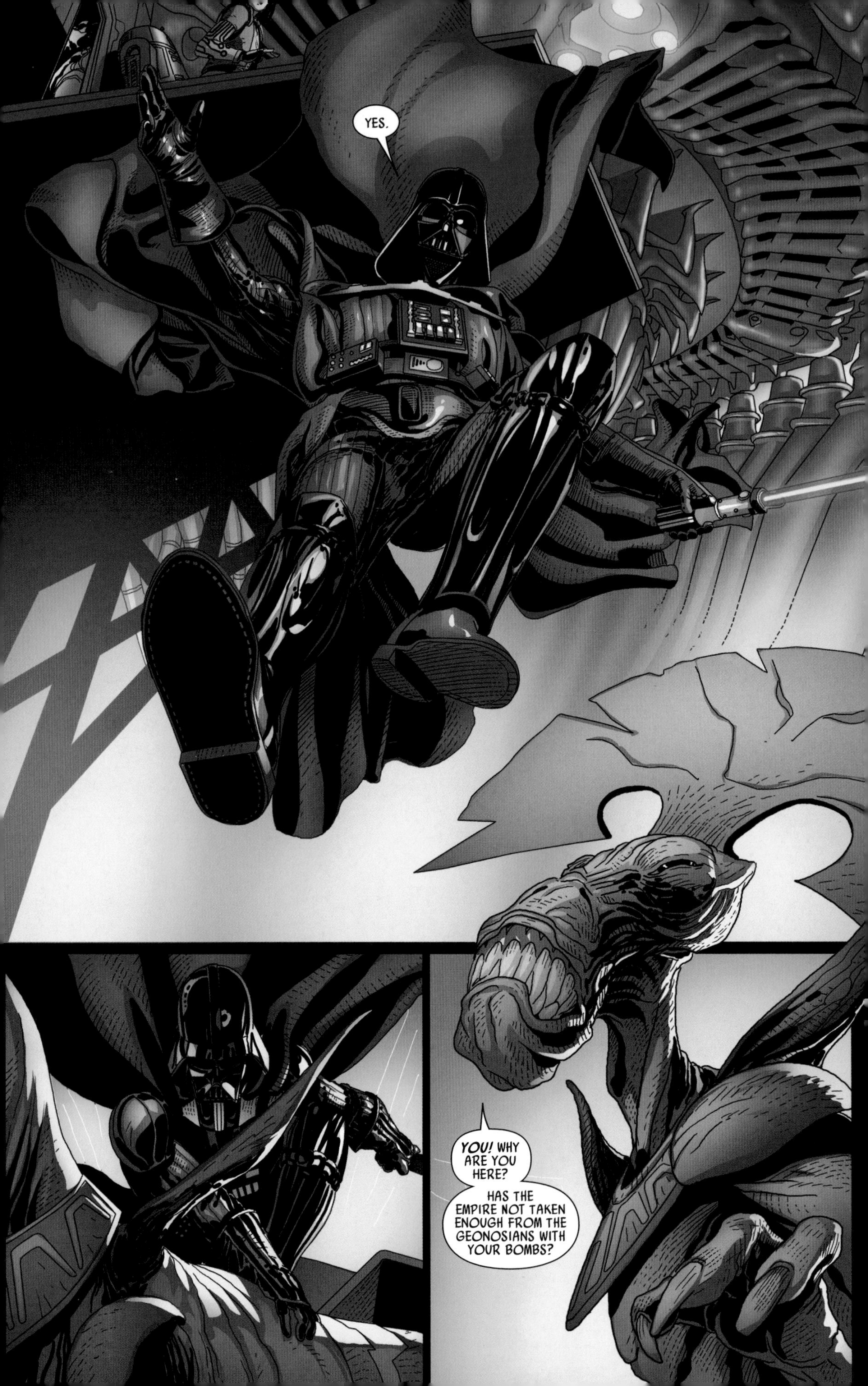

YES.
YOU! WHY ARE YOU HERE?
HAS THE EMPIRE NOT TAKEN ENOUGH FROM THE GEONOSIANS WITH YOUR BOMBS?

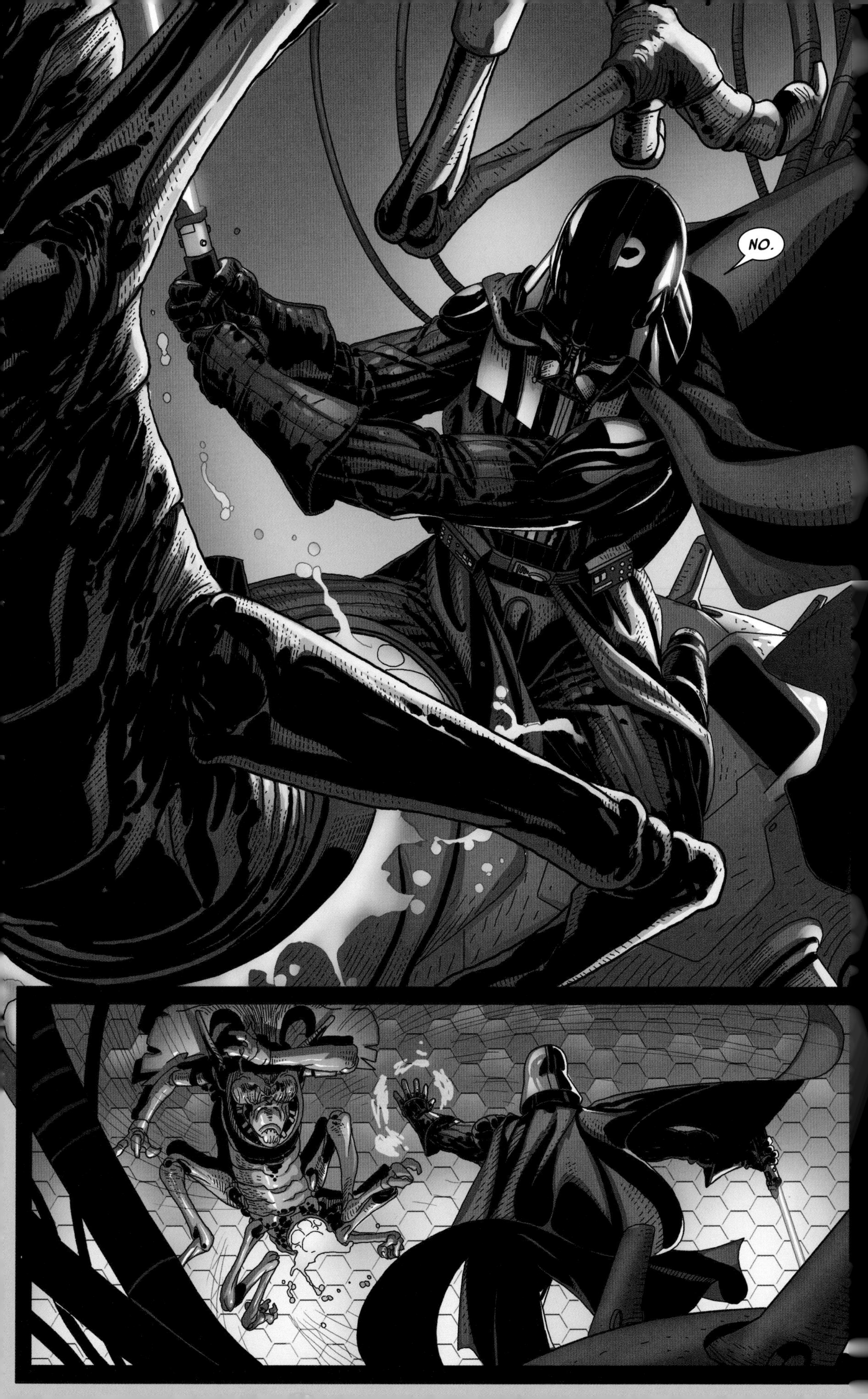
NO.

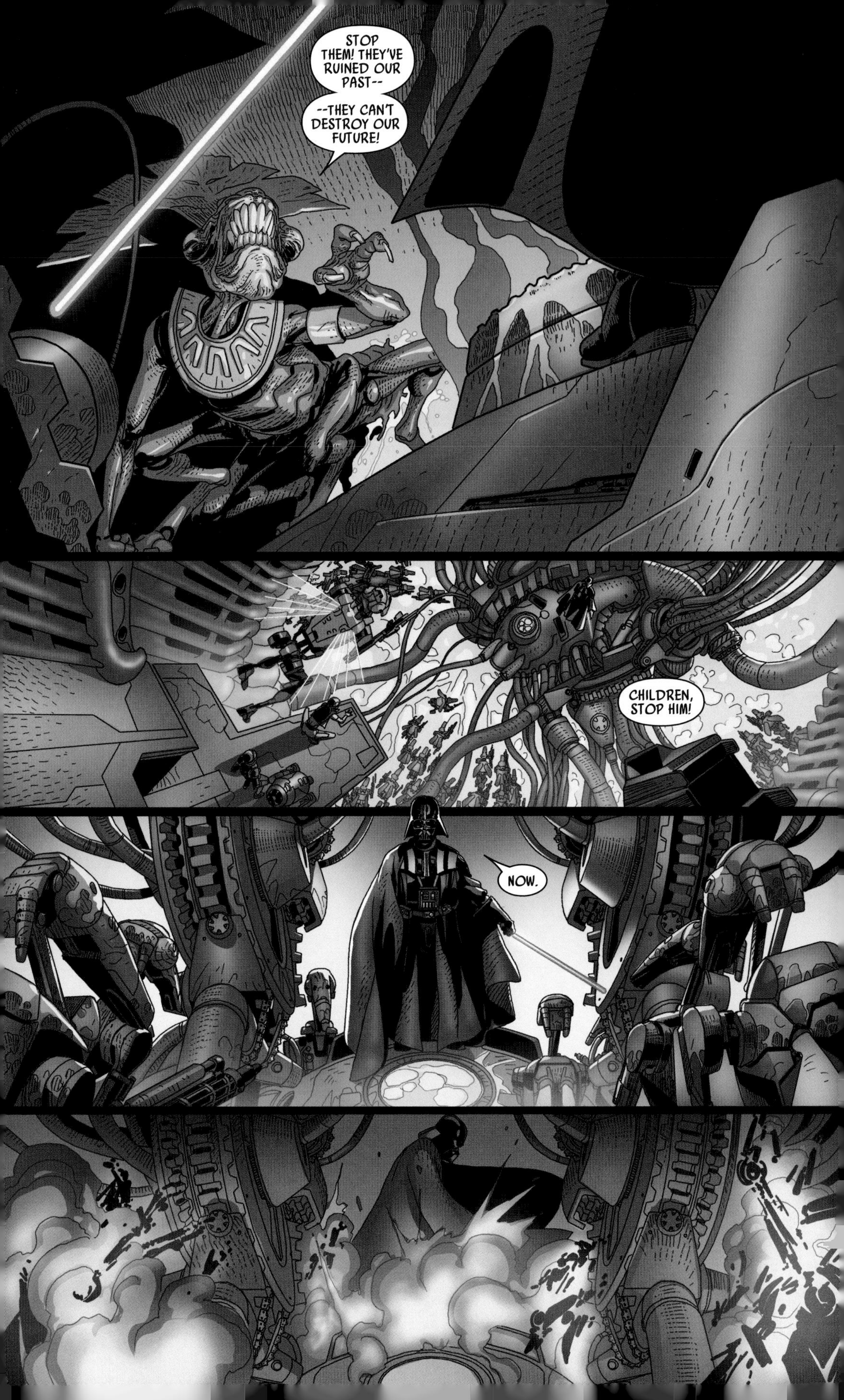
STOP THEM! THEY'VE RUINED OUR PAST--
--THEY CAN'T DESTROY OUR FUTURE!
CHILDREN, STOP HIM!
NOW.

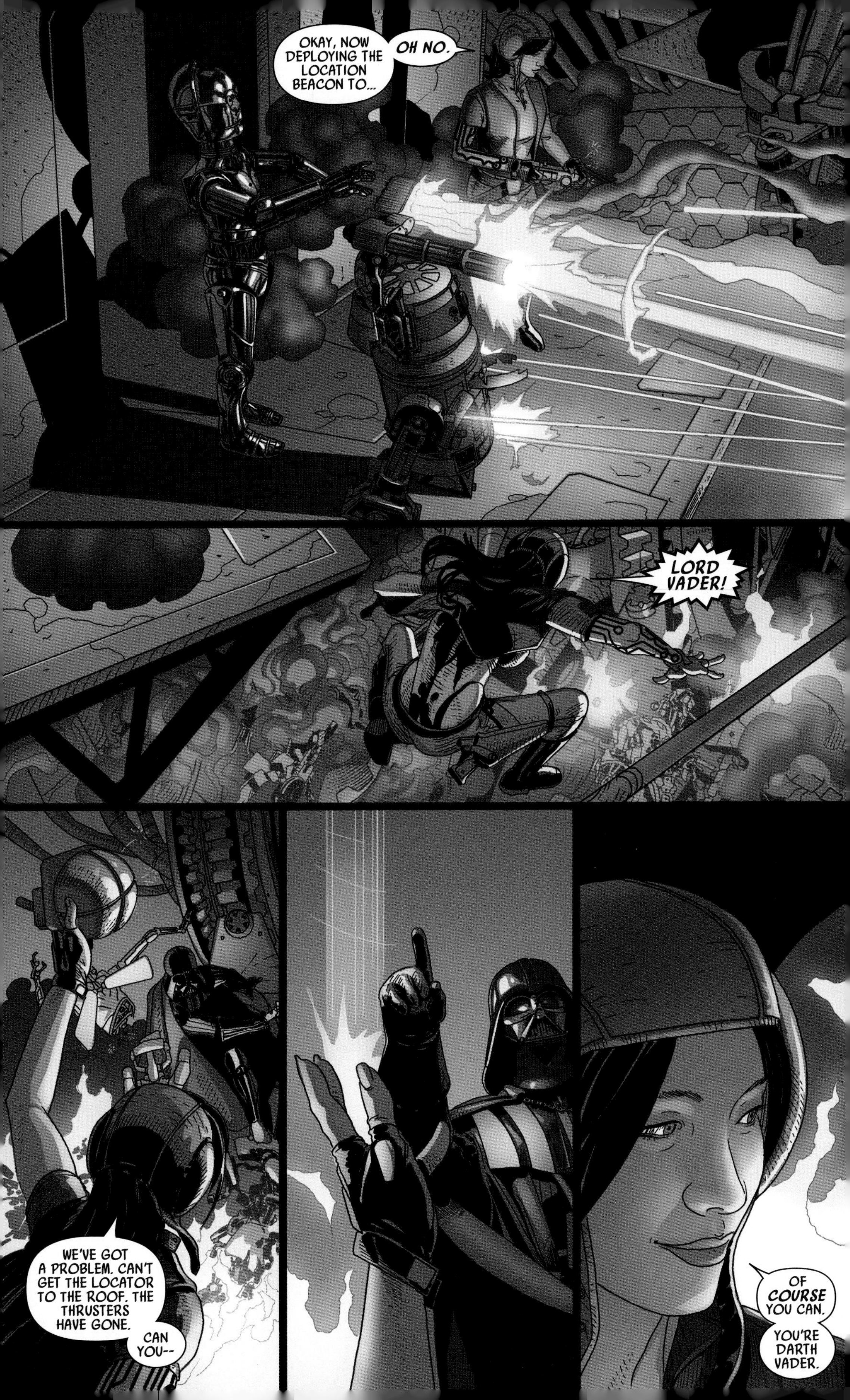
OKAY, NOW DEPLOYING THE LOCATION BEACON TO...
OH NO.
LORD VADER!
WE'VE GOT A PROBLEM. CAN'T GET THE LOCATOR TO THE ROOF. THE THRUSTERS HAVE GONE.
CAN YOU--
OF COURSE YOU CAN.
YOU'RE DARTH VADER.

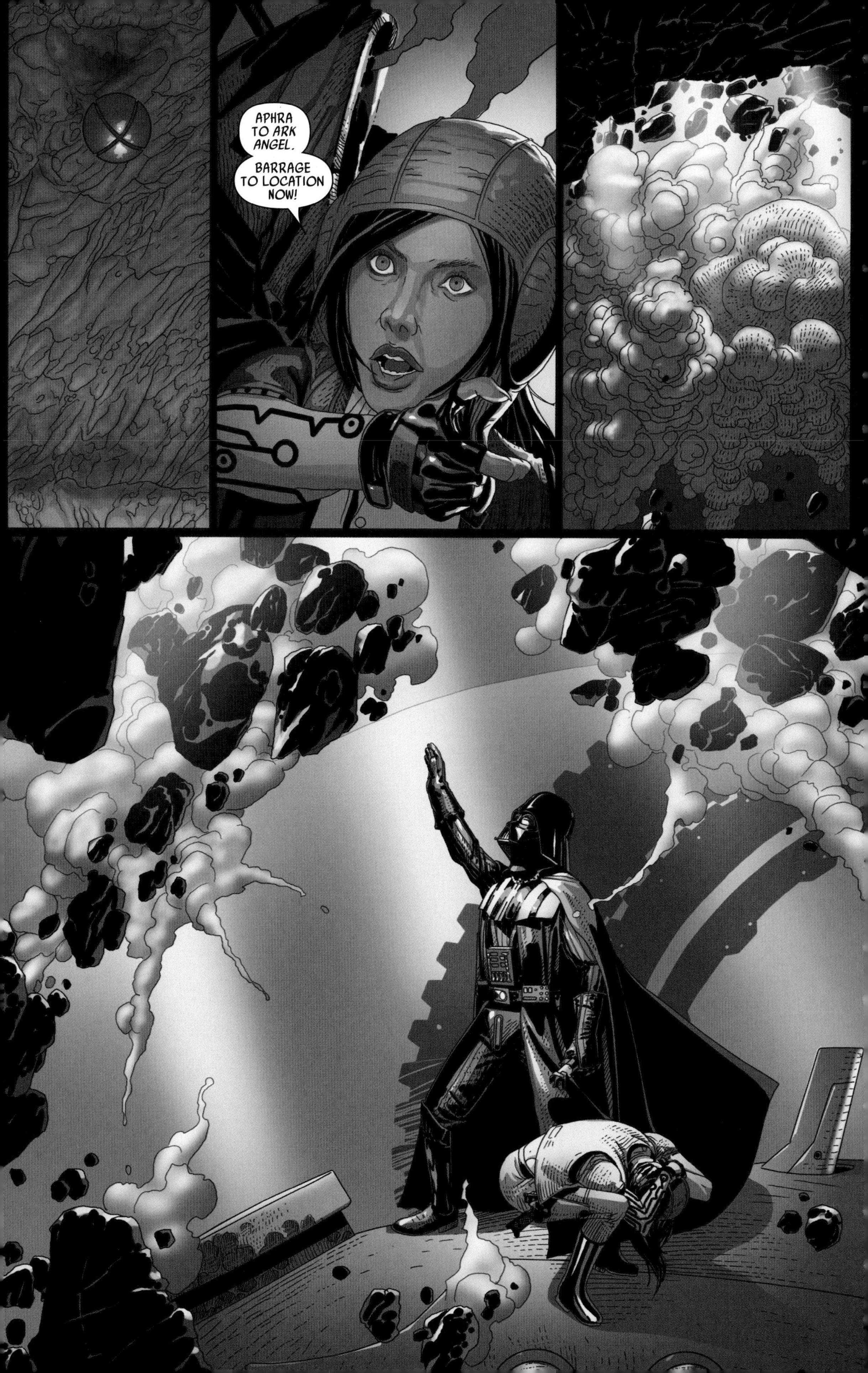
APHRA TO ARK ANGEL.
BARRAGE TO LOCATION NOW!

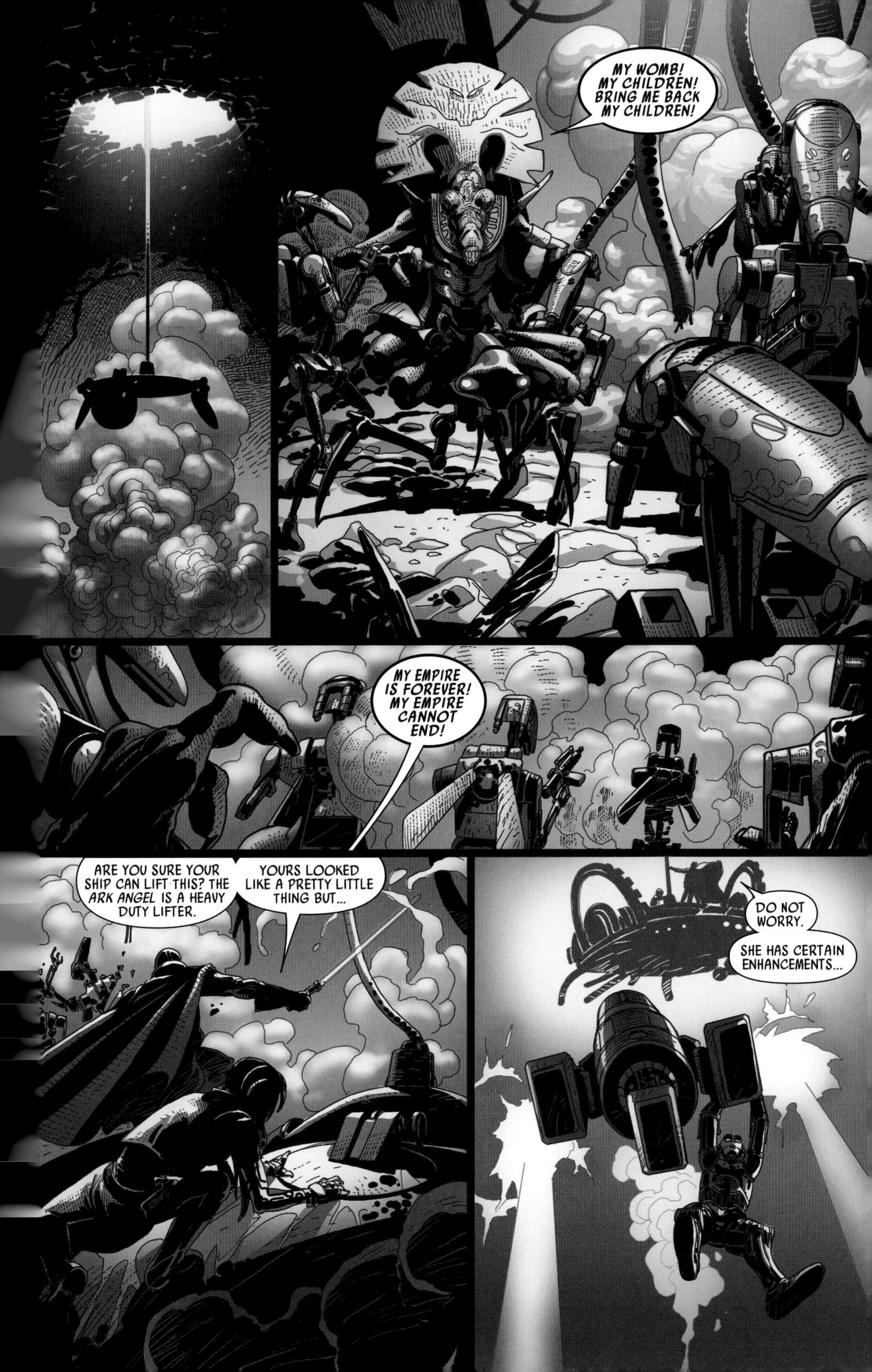
MY WOMB! MY CHILDREN! BRING ME BACK MY CHILDREN!
MY EMPIRE IS FOREVER! MY EMPIRE CANNOT END!
ARE YOU SURE YOUR SHIP CAN LIFT THIS? THE ARK ANGEL IS A HEAVY DUTY LIFTER.
YOURS LOOKED LIKE A PRETTY LITTLE THING BUT...
DO NOT WORRY.
SHE HAS CERTAIN ENHANCEMENTS...

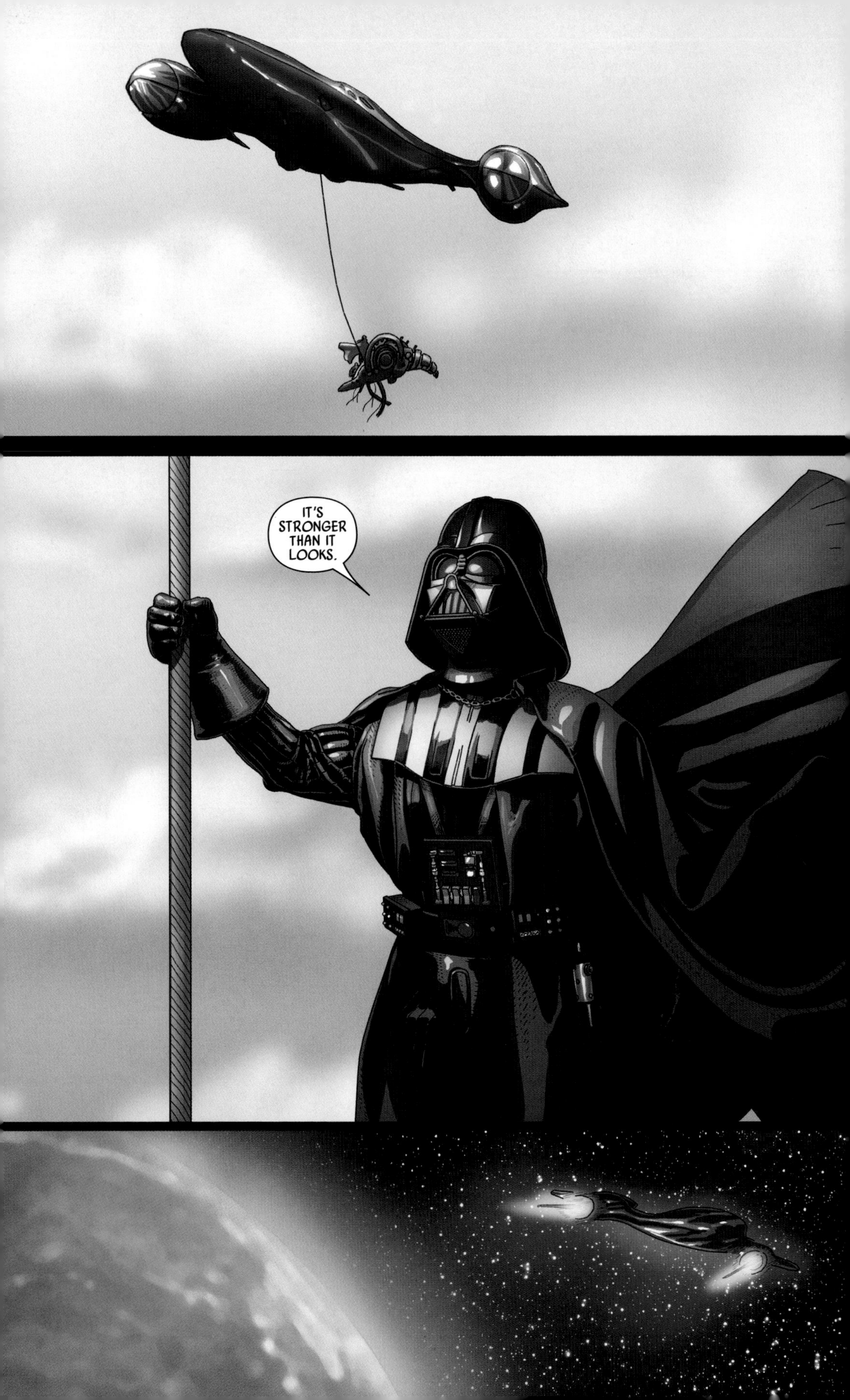
IT'S STRONGER THAN IT LOOKS.

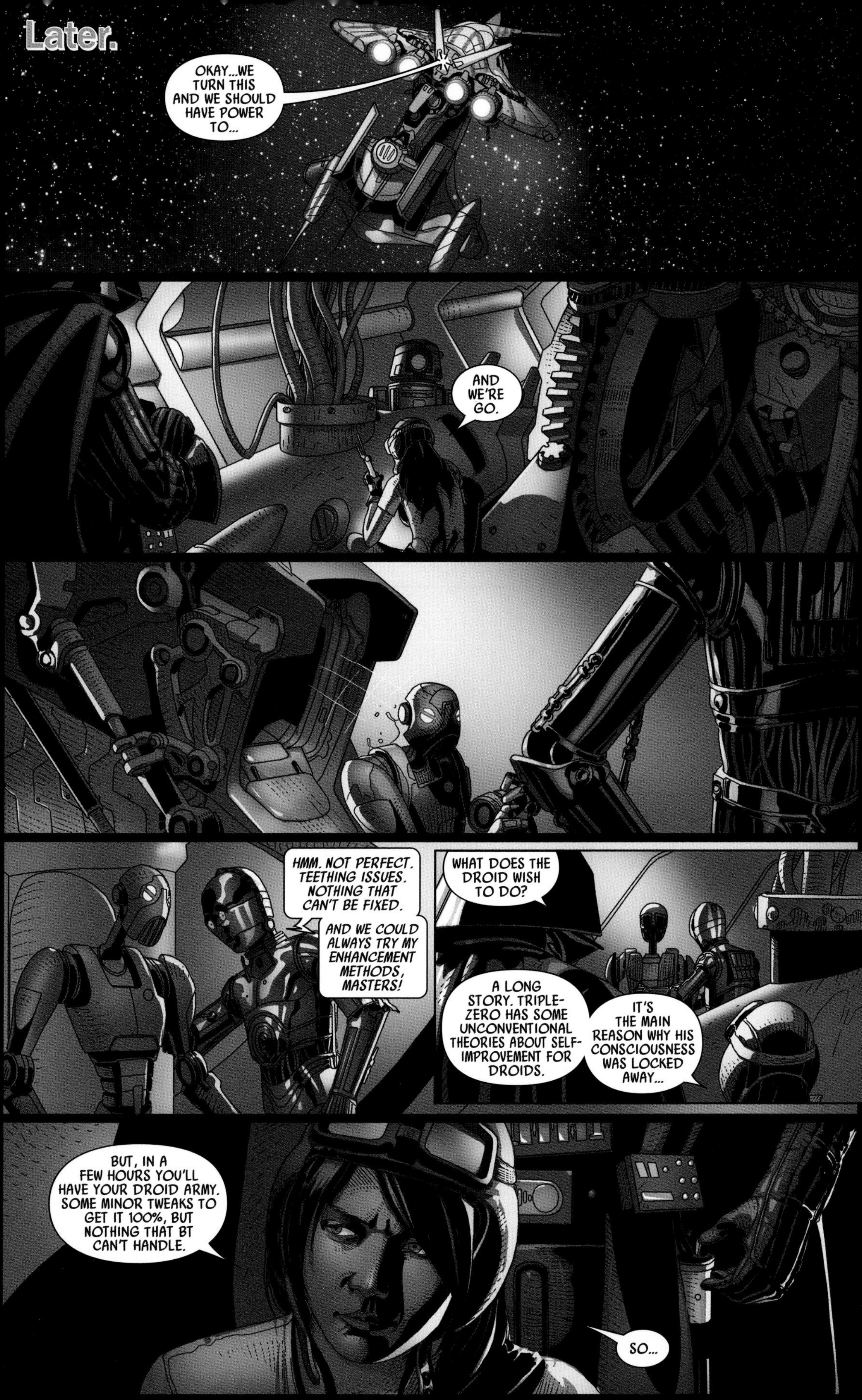
Later.
OKAY...WE TURN THIS AND WE SHOULD HAVE POWER TO...
AND WE'RE GO.
HMM. NOT PERFECT. TEETHING ISSUES. NOTHING THAT CAN'T BE FIXED.
AND WE COULD ALWAYS TRY MY ENHANCEMENT METHODS, MASTERS!
WHAT DOES THE DROID WISH TO DO?
A LONG STORY. TRIPLE-ZERO HAS SOME UNCONVENTIONAL THEORIES ABOUT SELF-IMPROVEMENT FOR DROIDS.
IT'S THE MAIN REASON WHY HIS CONSCIOUSNESS WAS LOCKED AWAY...
BUT, IN A FEW HOURS YOU'LL HAVE YOUR DROID ARMY. SOME MINOR TWEAKS TO GET IT 100%, BUT NOTHING THAT BT CAN'T HANDLE.
SO...

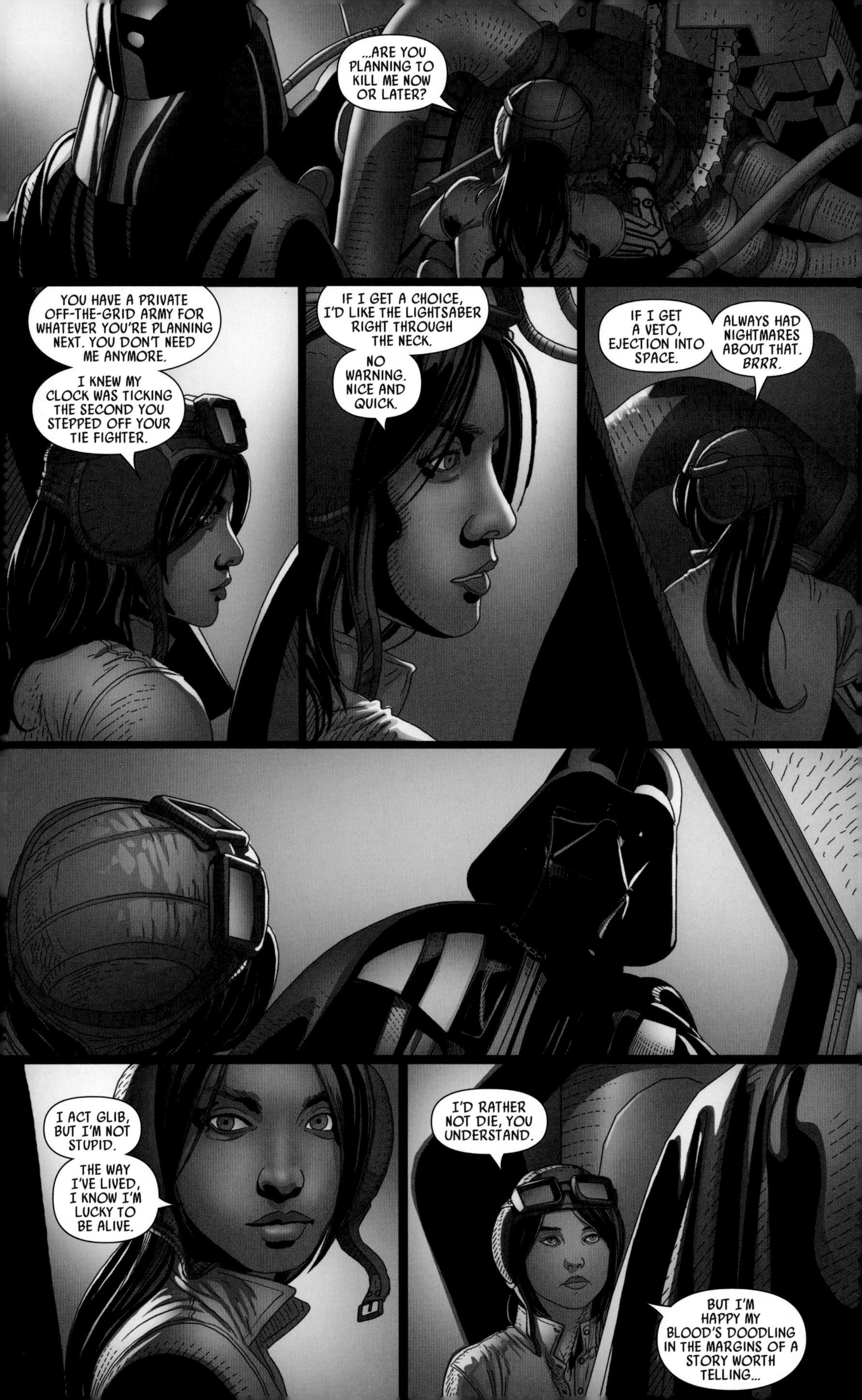
...ARE YOU PLANNING TO KILL ME NOW OR LATER?
YOU HAVE A PRIVATE OFF-THE-GRID ARMY FOR WHATEVER YOU'RE PLANNING NEXT. YOU DON'T NEED ME ANYMORE.
I KNEW MY CLOCK WAS TICKING THE SECOND YOU STEPPED OFF YOUR TIE FIGHTER.
IF I GET A CHOICE, I'D LIKE THE LIGHTSABER RIGHT THROUGH THE NECK.
NO WARNING. NICE AND QUICK.
IF I GET A VETO, EJECTION INTO SPACE.
ALWAYS HAD NIGHTMARES ABOUT THAT. BRRR.
I ACT GLIB, BUT I'M NOT STUPID.
THE WAY I'VE LIVED, I KNOW I'M LUCKY TO BE ALIVE.
I'D RATHER NOT DIE, YOU UNDERSTAND.
BUT I'M HAPPY MY BLOOD'S DOODLING IN THE MARGINS OF A STORY WORTH TELLING...

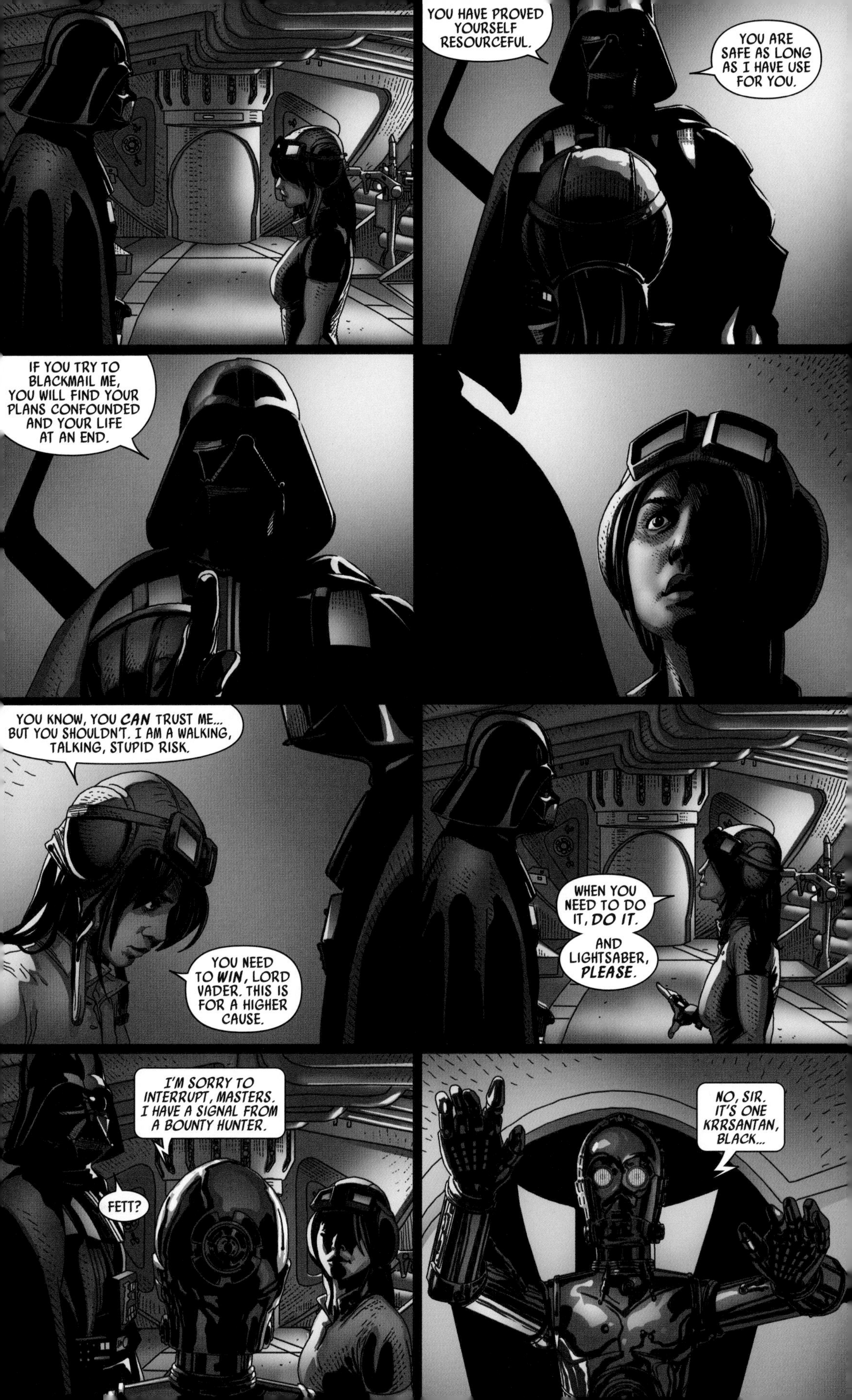
YOU HAVE PROVED YOURSELF RESOURCEFUL.
YOU ARE SAFE AS LONG AS I HAVE USE FOR YOU.
IF YOU TRY TO BLACKMAIL ME, YOU WILL FIND YOUR PLANS CONFOUNDED AND YOUR LIFE AT AN END.
YOU KNOW, YOU CAN TRUST ME... BUT YOU SHOULDN'T. I AM A WALKING, TALKING, STUPID RISK.
YOU NEED TO WIN, LORD VADER. THIS IS FOR A HIGHER CAUSE.
WHEN YOU NEED TO DO IT, DO IT.
AND LIGHTSABER, PLEASE.
I'M SORRY TO INTERRUPT, MASTERS. I HAVE A SIGNAL FROM A BOUNTY HUNTER.
FETT?
NO, SIR. IT'S ONE KRRSANTAN, BLACK...

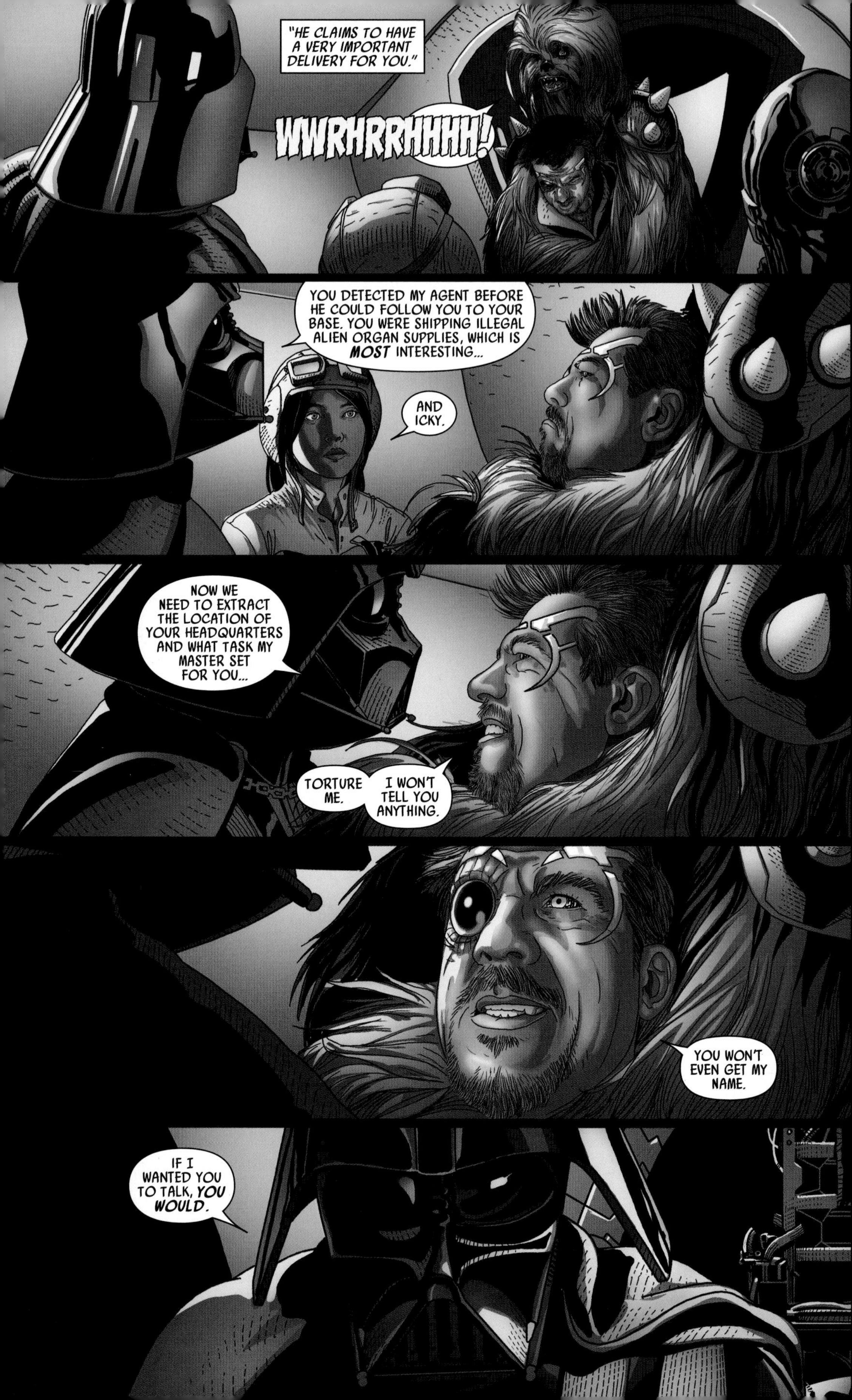
"HE CLAIMS TO HAVE A VERY IMPORTANT DELIVERY FOR YOU."
WWRHRRHHHH!
YOU DETECTED MY AGENT BEFORE HE COULD FOLLOW YOU TO YOUR BASE. YOU WERE SHIPPING ILLEGAL ALIEN ORGAN SUPPLIES, WHICH IS MOST INTERESTING...
AND ICKY.
NOW WE NEED TO EXTRACT THE LOCATION OF YOUR HEADQUARTERS AND WHAT TASK MY MASTER SET FOR YOU...
TORTURE ME.
I WON'T TELL YOU ANYTHING.
YOU WON'T EVEN GET MY NAME.
IF I WANTED YOU TO TALK, YOU WOULD.

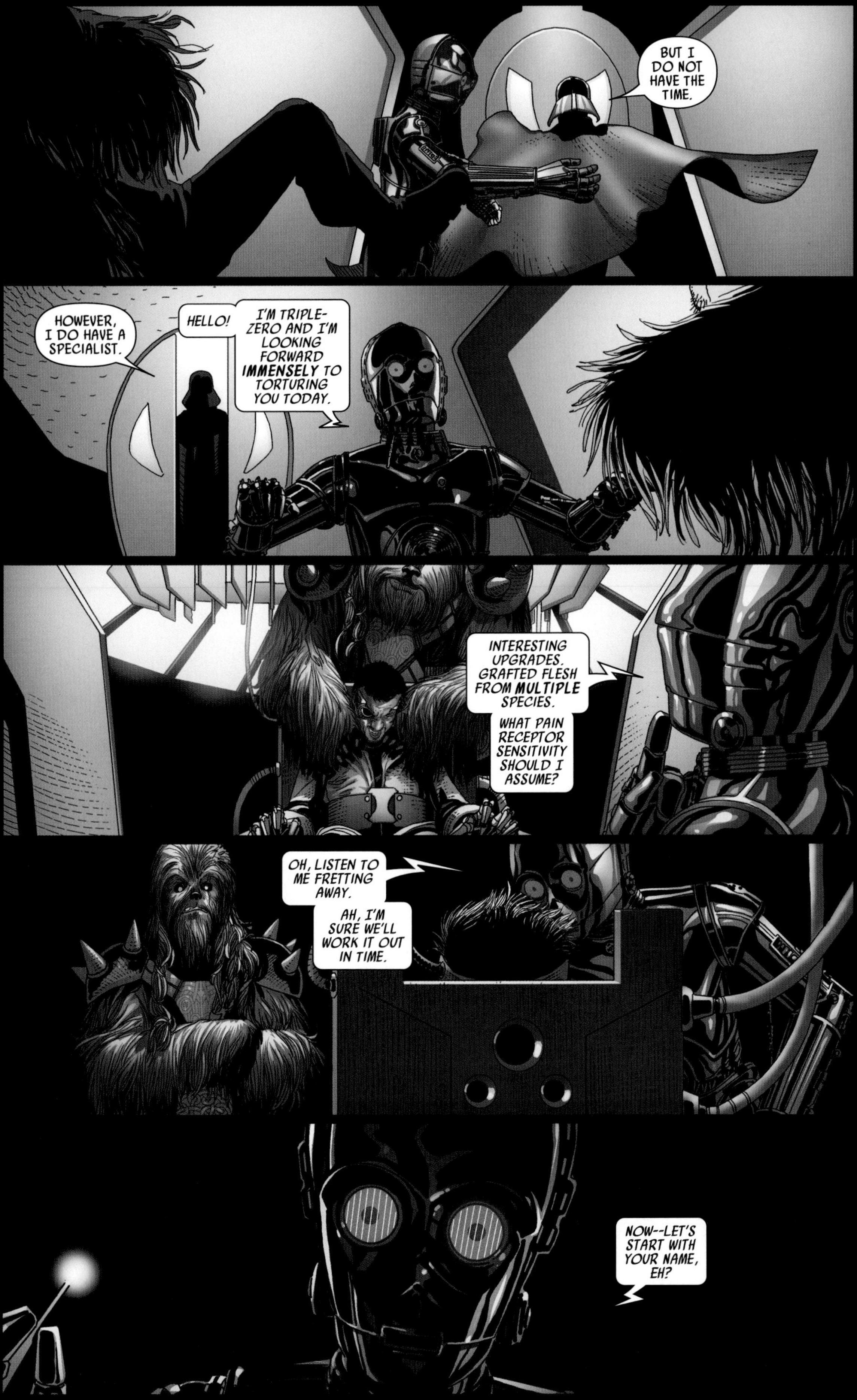
BUT I DO NOT HAVE THE TIME.
HOWEVER, I DO HAVE A SPECIALIST.
HELLO!
I'M TRIPLE-ZERO AND I'M LOOKING FORWARD IMMENSELY TO TORTURING YOU TODAY.
INTERESTING UPGRADES. GRAFTED FLESH FROM MULTIPLE SPECIES.
WHAT PAIN RECEPTOR SENSITIVITY SHOULD I ASSUME?
OH, LISTEN TO ME FRETTING AWAY.
AH, I'M SURE WE'LL WORK IT OUT IN TIME.
NOW--LET'S START WITH YOUR NAME, EH?

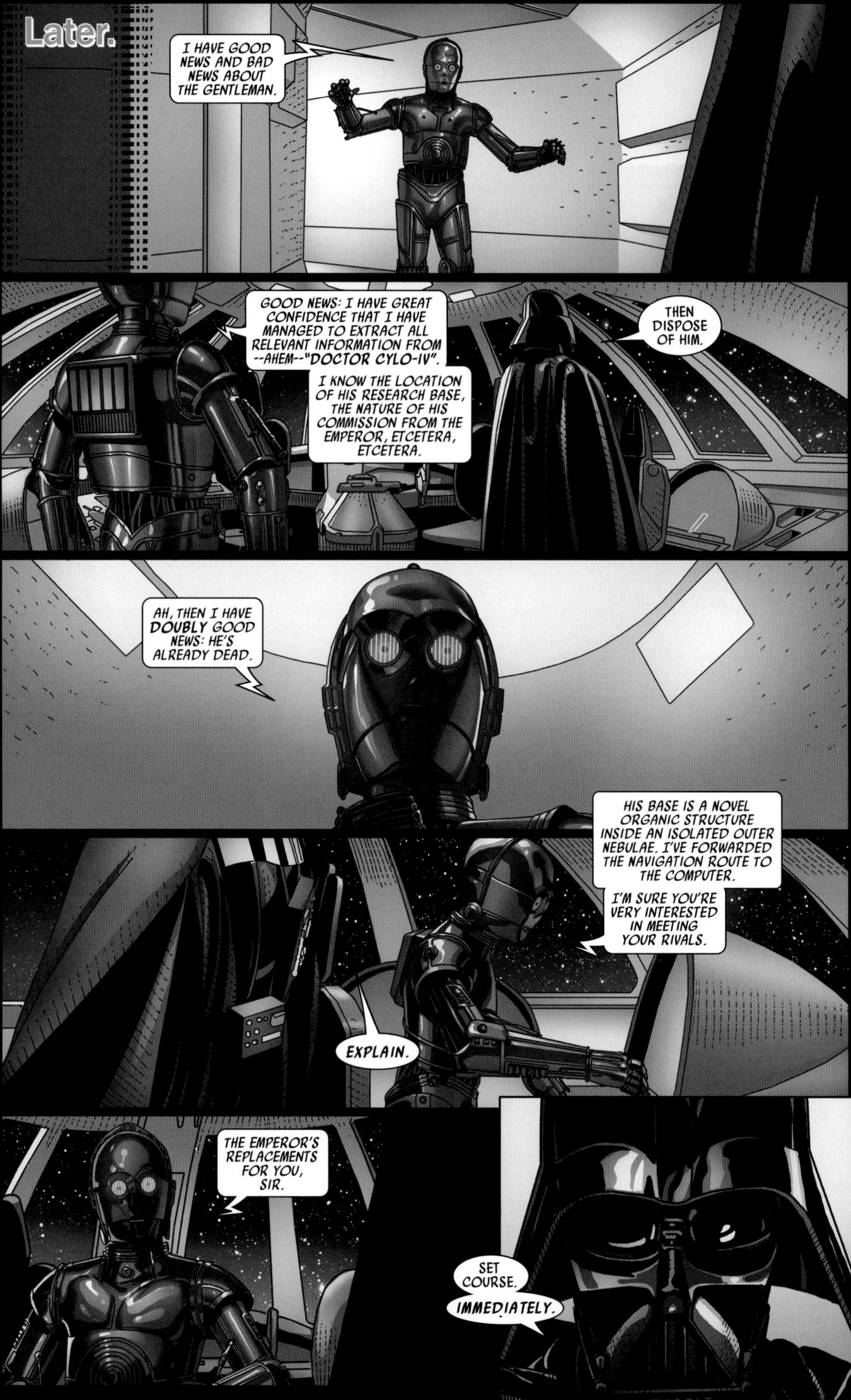
Later.
I HAVE GOOD NEWS AND BAD NEWS ABOUT THE GENTLEMAN.
GOOD NEWS: I HAVE GREAT CONFIDENCE THAT I HAVE MANAGED TO EXTRACT ALL RELEVANT INFORMATION FROM --AHEM--"DOCTOR CYLO-IV".
I KNOW THE LOCATION OF HIS RESEARCH BASE, THE NATURE OF HIS COMMISSION FROM THE EMPEROR, ETCETERA, ETCETERA.
THEN DISPOSE OF HIM.
AH, THEN I HAVE DOUBLY GOOD NEWS: HE'S ALREADY DEAD.
EXPLAIN.
HIS BASE IS A NOVEL ORGANIC STRUCTURE INSIDE AN ISOLATED OUTER NEBULAE. I'VE FORWARDED THE NAVIGATION ROUTE TO THE COMPUTER.
I'M SURE YOU'RE VERY INTERESTED IN MEETING YOUR RIVALS.
THE EMPEROR'S REPLACEMENTS FOR YOU, SIR.
SET COURSE.
IMMEDIATELY.

STAR WARS®

DARTH VADER

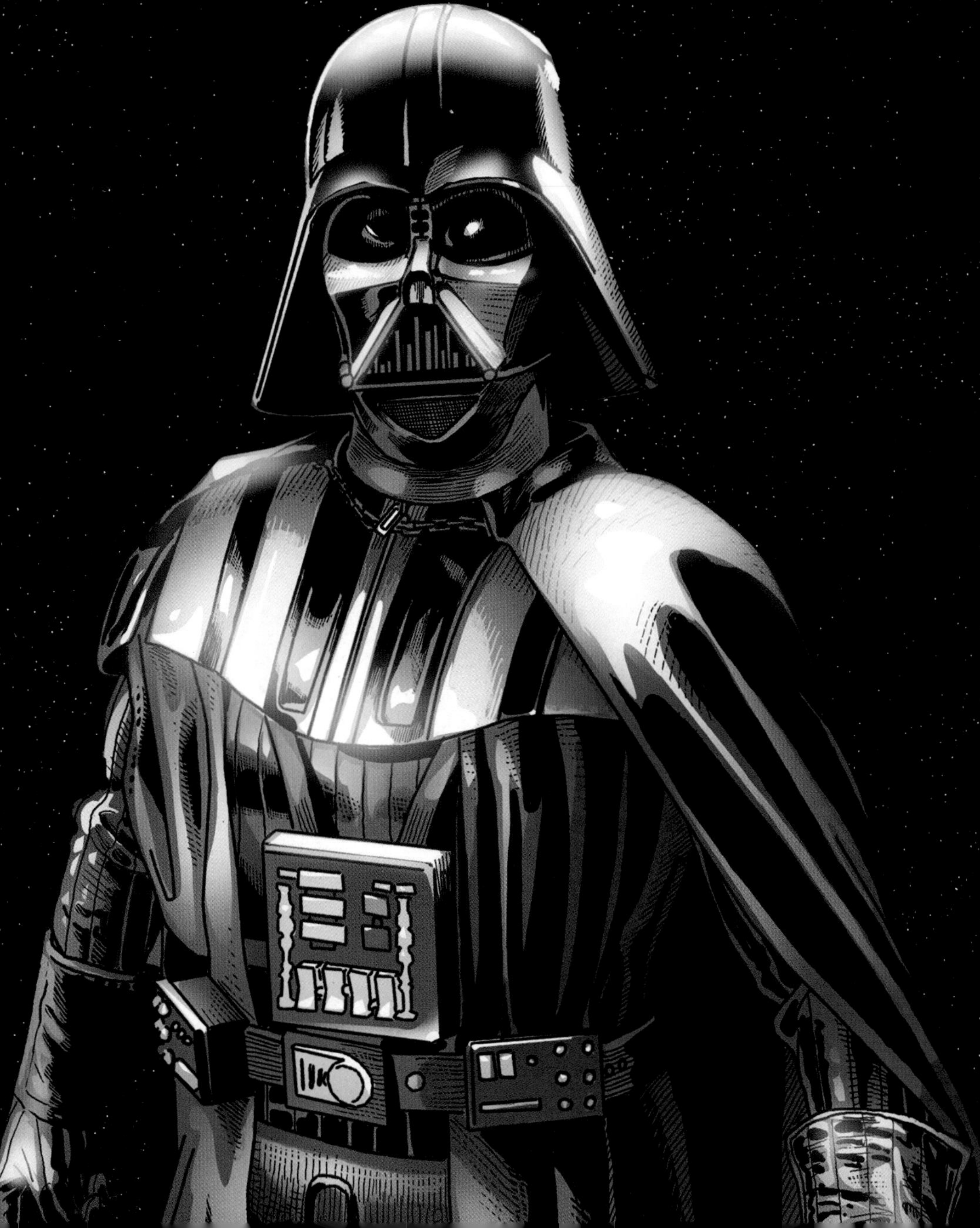

STAR WARS
DARTH VADER

COLLECT THEM ALL!

Set of 6 Hardcover Books ISBN: 978-1-61479-519-3

STAR WARS
STAR WARS
DARTH VADER
VADER: VOLUME 1
GILLEN LARROCA DELGADO

Hardcover Book ISBN
978-1-61479-520-9

STAR WARS
STAR WARS
DARTH VADER
VADER: VOLUME 2
GILLEN LARROCA DELGADO

Hardcover Book ISBN
978-1-61479-521-6

STAR WARS
STAR WARS
DARTH VADER
VADER: VOLUME 3
GILLEN LARROCA DELGADO

Hardcover Book ISBN
978-1-61479-522-3

STAR WARS
STAR WARS
DARTH VADER
VADER: VOLUME 4
GILLEN LARROCA DELGADO

Hardcover Book ISBN
978-1-61479-523-0

STAR WARS
STAR WARS
DARTH VADER
VADER: VOLUME 5
GILLEN LARROCA DELGADO

Hardcover Book ISBN
978-1-61479-524-7

STAR WARS
STAR WARS
VADER
VADER: VOLUME 6
GILLEN LARROCA DELGADO

Hardcover Book ISBN
978-1-61479-525-4

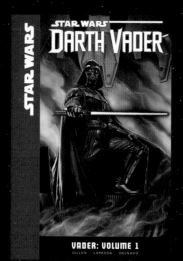

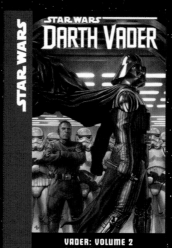

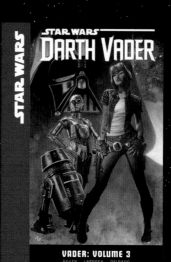

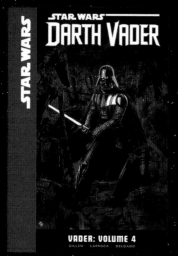

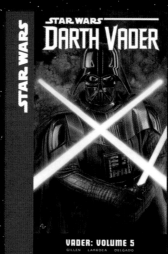

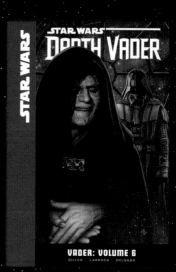